I0699782

Working Blue Press

First Edition

ISBN 978-1-967038-14-5 (Kindle)
ISBN 978-1-967038-15-2 (Print)

For all the men and women who love
great sex, great relationships, and a
damn good time.

Content

1 Night Swimming, *1*

2 Jenny Jones, 5

3 Pizza and My Best Friend, *14*

4 Last Minute Substitutions, *33*

5 Pool Party, *50*

6 Business or Pleasure?, *67*

Suggestions for Further Reading

Men Who Renovate Erotic Series
Books 1, 2, 3 and 4.

Follow Lacey Love on Amazon to keep abreast of new releases!

Night Swimming

Men Who Renovate Erotic Series

Book 2

1

Night Swimming

Danny had never been the type to lose control of anything. From his always perfectly coifed dark blonde hair to his carefully selected wardrobe, he was never out of line. And his buddies knew that.

So, for him to walk into the office this beautiful fall morning and try to explain how he ended up sleeping with seven sexy new college grads during his pool renovation was a tough task. It also explained the dumbfounded looks on their faces.

"Dude," Wolfe said. He ran his fingers through his dark hair and leaned back in his metal chair. "What the actual fuck?"

"I'm torn between 'what the fuck' and 'I'm so proud,'" Ben quipped. He cracked a smile and glanced at Jack.

"I'm not," Jack said. He crossed his arms over his worn sweatshirt. "I'm so fucking proud of you, man. Way to loosen up and enjoy life. Seven times."

"Well, three times," Danny said.

"I'm confused, I thought you said seven women?" Wolfe asked.

"I did," Danny said. "It was one woman the first time, plus her roommate, two women the second time, and three women the third time."

"Holy shit," Jack said. He grinned. "You're my fucking hero."

"Wait, were they the clients?" Ben asked.

"God no," Danny said. "The apartment complex is the client."

"So, the women lived there?" Wolfe asked.

"Two of them, yeah, roommates," Danny said. "The others were their college friends. A nurse, a dental hygienist, two former cheerleaders and a former volleyball player."

"Otherwise known as the fucking jackpot," Ben said.

They all laughed as Jack reached out his hand to give Ben a fist bump.

"I don't know, Wolfe hit the jackpot, I think," Danny said. He glanced at his childhood friend with a knowing grin.

"Yeah, how is Gina?" Jack asked.

"Amazing," Wolfe said.

"How long's it been now?" Ben followed up.

"Almost four months." Wolfe smiled as he held up four fingers. "Older woman. It's a sweet, sweet thing gentlemen."

They all chuckled as they turned back to Danny.

"Alright, man, we need the story," Ben said.

Jack nodded and raised an eyebrow at his friend. "Yeah, let's hear it."

Danny laughed as he leaned forward. "Alright, it all started with an offer for night swimming."

Jenny Jones

Danny couldn't believe his luck when Jenny Jones strode up to him wearing a black string bikini that showed off every inch of her beautiful five-foot, two-inch frame. If her blue eyes, blonde hair, and tight ass were going to be his view while he worked on this pool house renovation, he was in for the best week of his life.

"Hello again," he said.

"Hey," she cooed.

She had introduced herself earlier in the week when he'd been there to pick up the key and the check from the complex. Management wanted the pool house updated for fall so their tenants could use the area for football weekends and holiday parties.

Jenny had walked in just as he was about to leave and blocked his path in her cute little yellow sundress.

"I'm Jenny," she had said. "Jenny Jones."

"Danny," he had said. "You live here?"

"Yeah. Do you?"

She had grinned and he had thought her dimples were the cutest thing he'd ever seen.

"No. I'm doing some renovation work on the pool house. Get it ready for fall parties."

"Finally." She rolled her blue eyes. "It needs it."

A heated silence had passed between them as he'd eyed her adorable figure and she checked out his package, then she had said, "Well, see ya around."

She'd given him a sight to watch as she walked away, swinging those sweet little hips as she went. He had since come a few times to thoughts of grabbing her by those curves and thrusting inside of her while she came.

And now here she was in person, in a tiny, little bikini on a fall evening at a pool that was heated but still too chilly to enjoy.

"Water's cold," he said. He grinned as she sashayed up to him.

"I don't need it warm," she said seductively. She untied her bikini top and threw it aside as her beautiful, perky breasts with perfect little pink buds were in front of him. "My wet pussy is warm enough."

"Fuck," he whispered. This was straight out of a porn flick. But now it was happening in real life, and he wasn't sure what to do about it. No, that wasn't true, he knew exactly what to do about it. He wanted to rip off those bikini bottoms and fuck her right there. But he wasn't a fucking college student anymore—or a porn star. He was twenty-six years old, working full-time as a law clerk while he saved money to go to law school. Holy shit, he didn't even know how old this girl—woman—was.

As hard as his dick was, and as much as he wanted to fuck her, he reached down, picked up her top and handed it back to her.

"I can't." It's all he could get out.

She scoffed as she yanked her top out of his hand and covered her perfect breasts. "What? Why?"

She looked at him confused and even a little hurt. And he didn't want to hurt her while she was standing there vulnerable as all hell.

"No, I mean, you're beautiful, Jenny," he said. "It's Jenny, right? Jenny Jones?"

She softened a little that he knew her name. Of course he knew her name. He'd been yelling it in his shower since he met her, stroking his length until he came so hard he had no choice but to scream her name.

"I just," he paused. "I just, I don't know much about you."

"What do you wanna know?" She smiled then.

"Well, for starters, how old are you?"

She chuckled a little. "Oh," she said, almost as if reading his mind. "I'm legal, if that's your concern."

They both grinned as she turned away from him and put her top back on. She turned back around and her blue eyes were filled with humor.

"I'm 22," she said. "I just graduated in the spring. I went to school in Ohio. Ohio University in Athens."

"Party school," he quipped.

"Yeah, well, it was fun, for sure," she said. "But I went because it's got one of the best journalism programs in the country."

"You're a journalist?"

"I don't know what I am yet," she said. She shrugged as she crossed her arms to warm herself. "I'm working as a producer at the local TV station and hoping to get my break on-air at some point."

"You've got the face for it," he said. He quickly took off his sweatshirt and handed it to her. "Here. It's chilly."

"Thanks," she said quietly. She took it and slipped it over her head. It got stuck, so he stepped to her and grabbed the bottom, pulling it down as his lips came dangerously close to hers when the fabric slid over her head.

"Better?" he whispered.

She nodded as a warm feeling erupted in his pelvis and ran up his gut into his spine.

He finished pulling it down as she lowered her arms and smiled.

"I'm not really looking for anything serious," she said.

"Oh, okay."

"I just, I don't know how long I'm going to be in Little Palace, you know?"

"I get it," he said. "Me, either. I'm saving for law school, and I don't know where I may end up, either."

They nodded at each other, grinning as the heat between them became searing.

"Can I make you dinner tomorrow night?" she asked.

"Sure," he said.

"And by make you dinner, I mean, I'll order pizza after." She raised a playful eyebrow.

"Wow," he said. Holy shit, he liked her. He liked that she knew what she wanted—and how to get it. "I'm in."

"Good." She nodded across the parking lot to a condo at the edge. "I'm the end unit. 2310. Maybe around 7?"

He glanced over and saw a little Volkswagen bug, yellow, and cute. "Sure," he said. "That your bug?"

She nodded. "Yep."

"Cute."

"Thanks." When he turned back to her, she was on her tiptoes right in front of him. She kissed his cheek, and he could smell her warm, spicy perfume, minty toothpaste, and a vanilla-type shampoo. When she pulled back, he slid his hands up her arms to her throat and then in her hair. She grabbed his arms and locked eyes with him as he leaned down and lightly kissed her, then let her go.

"Tomorrow," he said quietly.

"Yeah." She bit her lip as she looked him right in the eyes, then turned and walked out of the pool area, through the pool house, across the lot, and to her condo. She paused at the door, looked at him, and smiled, then disappeared inside.

His cock could not have been any harder if he was stroking it himself.

Jenny-fucking-Jones.

He knew he was in for one hell of a ride. And for once in his life, he didn't want to control anything about what was going to happen between them.

For once in his life, he was just going to enjoy it.

3

Pizza and My Best Friend

As Danny knocked on Jenny's door at seven o'clock sharp, he felt a jolt of electricity go through him. He didn't know what to expect but he was grateful for that. He wanted to be surprised. He wanted something that was out of his control. He wanted something wild and free, like Jenny.

In high school, he had dated Marci for three years. In college it was Tamron for a year, then Stacy for a year, then Chloe for two years. He always did the responsible thing. He was always in a relationship. And that's what everyone expected of him, what he expected of himself.

And soon, he would be in law school, and then an attorney. And he'd be right back in that groove. Again. And what would he have to show for it? When had he ever really let go and just enjoyed life or sex or anything?

"Hey," Jenny said as she opened the door.

He had to catch his breath because holy fucking shit.

"Good God," he breathed.

"Exactly the reaction I was hoping for," she said. She grabbed his arm and pulled him inside, shutting the door behind him. He couldn't take his eyes off her.

She was wearing a lacy, princess blue bra with a matching garter set and no underwear. Her heels were the same color and three inches high. Her long blonde hair was curled and loose around her face and shoulders, tumbling down her chest and back, and framing her beautiful face. Her blue eyes were lovely and playful.

"You're…" He couldn't get it out of his mouth. He wasn't sure how to say thank you for being her, and for being playful, and for looking like that, and for taking the care to do so. And for doing it not just for him but for herself. He could see she was happy to see him, too, and hopeful for him to give her as much as she was giving him.

"You're beautiful, Jenny," he finally said. "Seriously."

His sincerity must have caught her off-guard because she blinked back surprise.

"Oh, thank you," she said quietly. "You look handsome."

He grinned. He had tried to meet her expectations. He'd shaved and groomed every part of his body, including his cock and balls, making sure every stray hair was gone and it was ready for her. If he was going to do this, he wanted to enjoy it and he wanted her to enjoy it, too.

He took a step toward her and slid his hands into her hair, tipping her face up to his and touching his nose to hers, then his lips to hers, then locked eyes with her.

"You're so fucking sexy," he said.

"God, I want you," she whispered.

His hand grabbed her hair and pulled just a little to tip her head back as he kissed her deeply while his other hand slid down her body, stopping at her breasts and sliding one hand into her bra. He thumbed her nipple as a little moan escaped her lips.

That sound made his cock come to life and harden immediately. She tasted so good as his tongue slid deep in her mouth and out again, going from soft and gentle to deep and urgent. He squeezed her nipple, then moved his hand further south.

"Yes," she panted as his kiss relented and moved down her throat to her breast, taking the nipple into his mouth as his fingers found her wet slit.

"Fuck, Jenny, you're so wet," he moaned.

"Just for you, baby," she said. Her hands found his hair and helped guide his mouth to her sweet spot.

He moaned as he smelled her sexiness, a delicious sweet scent he wanted to taste. He pulled off his shirt and tossed it aside as he grabbed her ass and dove between her legs with an animal instinct he hadn't felt in ages.

"Yes, Danny, yes!"

She tasted like the most intoxicating sweetness that had ever touched his tongue. He licked her pussy lips up and down, stopping to swirl his tongue around her clit as she moaned with pleasure.

"Sixty-nine me, baby," she ordered.

"Fuck yes," he said. He stood up and together they ripped the rest of his clothes and shoes off, then her bra, tossing it all aside as she led him to the living room where she'd set up a comfortable, blanketed area near the fireplace, which was crackling with heat.

"Lay down," she directed.

He did as he was told and got comfortable on the blankets and pillows, rubbing his cock as she positioned her beautiful pussy and ass above him. She briefly looked over her shoulder with a smile, then gently lowered herself down, positioning her pussy near his mouth and her own mouth at his cock.

"Fuck yes," he moaned. He grabbed her ass and pulled her pussy right on top of his mouth, digging in and eating her wildly as she slid his cock in her mouth.

He could hear her moaning as she licked his tip, teasing him, then taking him almost fully in her mouth while she stroked the base.

"Jenny, fuck," he said as he paused for a moment to enjoy her handiwork. Fuck she could suck cock. "Suck me, baby, yes."

"Mmmm," she moaned, pulling his cock out of her mouth. "Baby you're so fucking hard."

She swallowed him again and again as he started to feel his orgasm grow. He tasted her again, driving his tongue inside her as she groaned. He took the moment to give her a light slap on the ass.

"Yes!" she screamed. Now that he knew she liked it and wanted it, he gave her another slap on the ass, this time a little harder. "Again!"

He wanted to give it to her again, but he didn't want to hurt her, either. He held back a little and gave her a slap on the cheek as he sucked her clit.

"Fuck," she moaned. "I'm getting close."

"I need to fuck you," he panted.

She slid off him and sat on the carpet with her legs spread. "How do you want me, baby?"

"Just like that." He sat up and crawled to her, grabbing her hips and sliding her to him. He positioned himself between her legs, his leaking tip teasing her entrance. When she moaned, he trailed his eyes up her gorgeous body to her steamy stare.

"Fuck," he whispered. She really was beautiful. Her blue eyes were clear and steady, filled with want. There was no back-up on her, no apologies, just simple pleasure. That would change for her someday. At some point, she'd want more from some man she loved and wanted a future with. And that man would give it to her because of those blue eyes and what was behind them. But that man wasn't him. And it wasn't today.

Still, he never wanted to be "that asshole guy she slept with." He wanted to be "that awesome fucking guy she slept with that maybe, someday…"

He smiled at her then and slid his hands and body down hers, laying her back and softly kissing her. He looked into her eyes as she smiled back at him.

"Jenny Jones," he whispered.

"Danny," she said quietly. She slid her hands down his back and grabbed his ass. "Fuck me."

He grinned as he slid deep inside her.

"Yes," she moaned. "Fuck, you're huge."

"You like that, baby?" he asked. He buried his mouth in her neck and kissed it up to her mouth, thrusting and sliding his cock in and out of her slick pussy.

"Yes," she moaned. "Yes, more!"

He lifted off her, grabbing her thighs and pulling her pussy even closer, driving his cock deep inside.

"Like that?"

"Harder!" she panted.

He pulsed and pushed harder as his orgasm started to rise.

"I'm gonna come," she yelled.

"Come," he ordered. "Come hard, Jenny!"

"I'm coming," she yelled. He could feel her pussy squeeze around his cock, and it drove him over the edge as he pulled out and came hard and fast all over her perky tits and toned stomach.

He jerked his cock in euphoria as his salty release lay wet and thick on her body. She moaned as she came down from her orgasm and smiled at him.

"Fuck," he said quietly as he finished, and his heart rate started to drop. She brought her hand up and ran a delicate finger through his come, then put it to her mouth and sucked.

"Mmmm," she said delicately. "You taste good."

"Holy shit," he breathed. He leaned down and kissed her as a knock at the door interrupted them.

"Oh, dinner," she said. She gave him a wicked grin. "And dessert."

"What?" he asked. He knew he could expect a few pleasant surprises with her. Maybe this was one?

"Why don't you go get the door?" she teased.

"Uh, sure," he said. He started to look around for his clothes.

"Baby, you don't need clothes."

He eyed the expression on her face and smiled as he stood and started to walk to the door. Yes, this is exactly what he wanted. What he needed. He could already feel the knot inside his gut loosening, letting go a little bit. He opened the door.

"Holy fuck," he whispered.

"Nope, not holy fuck, holy Madeline," she said. Her tall, lithe frame was adorned in nothing but a simple little red string bikini. She was holding a pizza, and her dark hair was cut short in a bob around her face. Her eyes were hazel, and her smile was dazzling. "Are you gonna let me in?"

"Uh, yeah," he said. He stepped aside as she walked past him, her light citrus scent filling his lungs as he shut the door. He turned to face her, and she quickly set the pizza down on the little island in the kitchen, then walked back to him and slowly untied and pulled off her bikini.

He let out a breath as her breasts tumbled out, big and bouncy with her nipples at attention.

"Taste me," she directed. He glanced quickly at Jenny, who was now on her side and watching them. She smiled at him.

"Mads is my roommate. Suck her titties, baby," Jenny said, her heated stare watching them as she reached between her legs and started masturbating.

"Fuck," he panted as his cock got hard again. He walked to Madeline and pulled one beautiful titty into his mouth while he fondled the other one.

"Mmmm, yes," she moaned. Her hands found his hair and pulled on it. "Eat my pussy."

"Fuck yes," he said. He kissed his way down her stomach to her perfectly waxed and shaved folds as he dove between her legs with a hunger he'd repressed almost his whole life. "Fuck."

He licked and sucked her clit, tasting her wetness as he slid up and down her lips.

"More," she ordered.

He slid his fingers deep inside her as he tasted her over and over, the sweet musky flavor coating his tongue and mouth.

"You taste amazing," he breathed.

"Let me suck your cock." She grabbed his hair and pulled on it as he rose. She put her hands on his chest and walked him backward to a kitchen chair, forcing him down in it. She smiled as she got on her knees and slid her hands up his thighs.

"Baby," he moaned. "Fuck yes."

She slowly licked the pre-come off his tip and then started to pull his hard cock into her delicious mouth.

"God yes," he panted. He slid his hands in her hair, gently directing her mouth as she moaned. He peered over at Jenny, who was now walking toward them, naked and beautiful. "Jenny."

She got to him and kissed him deeply as Madeline sucked his cock deep and steady, grabbing his thick shaft as his orgasm started to build again.

Jenny pulled back.

"No, wait," he said.

"Nope," she said, slapping his hand away as she walked backward to the island and slid onto it, spreading her legs wide. "Madeline."

She sang her friend's name in a flirty way as the brunette stopped sucking his cock and turned her attention to Jenny's sweet pussy.

"Yum," she said excitedly. Madeline got off her knees and walked to Jenny, dipping her head between Jenny's legs and licking her pussy.

"Fuck yes," Jenny moaned. "Lick me just like that, Mads."

Jenny grabbed Madeline's hair and roughly directed her in eating her pussy as Danny grabbed his cock and started jerking it. He couldn't believe what he was watching, but he fucking loved it.

"Danny," Jenny moaned. "Fuck her."

Fuck. Yes. He stood up and walked up behind Madeline, first leaning down and licking her pussy, then positioning himself between her legs and teasing her entrance with his tip.

"Yes," she moaned. She glanced over her shoulder and smiled, then went back to licking Jenny's pussy as Jenny moaned and squirmed.

Jenny locked eyes with him as he slid the tip in Madeline.

"Do it," she panted. "Fuck her!"

He quickly slid his cock deep inside Madeline's tight little pussy as she moaned with pleasure.

"Harder," Jenny ordered.

He pounded the fuck out of Madeline as she gripped Jenny's ass and dove deeper in her pussy.

"I'm gonna come," Jenny panted.

"Come!" he ordered. He reached around and rubbed Madeline's clit as she squirmed with pleasure.

"I'm coming!" Jenny cried out as her body convulsed with wave after wave of pleasure. Madeline cried out, "I'm coming, too!"

"I'm coming," he groaned. He rubbed Madeline's clit faster as she came, her pussy clenching around his cock.

It felt so good he almost came inside of her. He was tempted to do it, but he couldn't. He quickly pulled out and came all over her back, jerking out every last bit of salty release he could muster.

"Fuck," he panted.

They all glanced at each other and chuckled as they started to come down from the sexual high.

"Did you like that, baby?" Jenny purred.

She grinned at him as Madeline looked over her shoulder and smiled.

"Yeah, did you like it?" Madeline prompted.

"You have no idea," he said. He quickly grabbed a paper towel from the roll on the counter and wiped off Madeline's back so she could stand.

"Well," Madeline said as she faced him and trailed her finger down his chest. "How about we eat some pizza, and then try something new? I have a few ideas."

He slid his hands into her hair and kissed her deeply, Jenny's pussy on her tongue driving him wild.

"Fuck yes," he said. He glanced at Jenny and smiled. "You up for more?"

"Oh baby," she quipped. "You have no idea."

He let out a deeply held breath and smiled.

This is exactly what he needed, and a little bit more.

4

Last Minute Substitutions

Danny had spent the day renovating the pool house while wildly anticipating the night. Jenny and Madeline had invited him back, and he wanted nothing more than to be with them again, passionate and enjoying the moment. He'd never let go so fully and he was loving every second of it.

"Looking good."

Danny turned and saw the apartment manager, Shannon, a tall woman, lovely, about his age. She had long auburn hair and bright green eyes.

"Thanks," he said. He peered around at his work. He'd taken out a wall and opened up the seating area, replaced the flooring from stone tiles to a warm hardwood. The kitchenette area had new stainless-steel appliances and the first coat of paint was drying to a smart, neutral cream.

"When do you start the outside stuff?" she asked.

"Oh, the tiki torches?" he said. He winked as she laughed.

"Gas torches, yes, and the fire pit," she said. "I think our tenants will love it."

"I think they will, too," he said. He glanced at her for a second. "Did you have anything to do with all this work?"

"I suggested it, yeah," she quipped. She shrugged. "And I'm the one that found your business."

"Found us?" Oh no. Hopefully she hadn't heard about Wolfe's escapades and that's why she was here now. Not that he wouldn't fuck her, she was beautiful, but he hoped their reputation was

spreading because they were good
and not just sexy.

"Google," she said. She raised
her eyebrows. "You've got an
almost five-star rating. That's
impressive. And I saw the photos
on the website. Your before and
after albums. You guys seem to
really know what you're doing."

"Oh, thanks," he said. She
emanated kindness and something
else he couldn't quite put his finger
on. Her delicate features were
incredibly feminine, and her
professional clothing was sitting
right at the border of sexy without
overdoing it. "How long have you
been here?"

"About a year. I graduate next
spring."

"Just now graduating?"

"Yeah, I went to community
college," she said quietly. A blush
slid across her cheeks. "It's just me
and my grandma. It's all I could

afford. But I'll have a business degree. I want to get into real estate management."

"Oh, very cool," he said. He didn't want her to feel embarrassed, which she seemed to. "A lot of people wouldn't even bother to go to school if they couldn't afford it. That's impressive."

"Thanks," she said. She smiled brightly at him as she tucked a long strand of hair behind her ear. "Well, I'll let you get back to it."

"Okay," he said. She grinned as she turned and walked away. He eyed her ass, perky and firm, as she did. She did a quick over-the-shoulder-glance at him and blushed as he smiled. Then she disappeared into her office.

"Huh," he said under his breath. He turned and looked around. It was time to wrap up and head over to Jenny's. His cock stiffened at just the thought of what was to come. He cleaned up, put everything away, loaded his truck, and drove the short distance to her door and parked. There was a cute little Jeep in the spot where Jenny's bug had been.

"Is that hers, too?" She had told him to just come on in when he was done, and they'd help him in the shower once he arrived. He grinned as he climbed out of his truck and walked to the door. He knocked to announce his arrival and then walked in. He could hear the shower running and smiled as he took off his socks and boots at the door.

He walked further into the condo, noting more detail now that he wasn't buried deep in Jenny's sweet pussy. It was very modern, blacks and whites, sparse details, and a little messy. Dishes in the sink, things out of place. Beauty magazines were lying across what looked like an Ikea coffee table.

He stripped off his shirt as he got to the bedroom and threw it on the bed. The steam was floating out of the master bathroom, and he could see two females going at it through the glass door. His cock got immediately hard.

"Fuck yes," he whispered.

He stripped off his pants and boxers and stepped out of them as he moved to the bathroom.

"Ladies?" he said loudly. He didn't want to scare them.

The glass door opened, and a beautiful brunette peeked out.

"Hi, Danny," she cooed.

"Oh fuck," he said, stepping back quickly and covering his junk. "Who are you?"

"We're your last-minute substitutions," said another sexy voice. This time a petite redhead poked her head out and smiled at him. "Jenny had to work a late shift and Madeline had to help her brother. So, they called us, and here we are."

"Yeah, we heard you're amazing in bed," said the brunette. "We want a turn."

"I don't…" he said as he assessed the situation.

"Oh, we're legal," the brunette laughed. "Jenny warned us you'd be hesitant about that. We went to college with her. We're both 22."

"I'm Gigi," said the redhead.

"And I'm Bree," said the brunette.

"Come fuck us," Gigi purred. "Pleeeease."

The two opened the door all the way and started rubbing each other up and down. Their bodies were beautiful. Gigi was a little heavier and curvy with big, beautiful breasts, while Bree was athletic and muscled. They were both taller than

Jenny, and equally confident and sexy.

Bree moaned as Gigi started sucking her titties, then dropped to her knees and slid her tongue between Bree's legs. Bree flicked a hot stare at Danny, holding out her hand for him to join.

"Fuck it," he whispered. He wanted surprises. He got it.

He reached out and took her hand, stepping into the shower and closing the door behind him. He rinsed off under the stream of hot water, then turned and pulled Bree into a deep kiss as Gigi licked her wetness.

Danny dropped his mouth to her breasts, sucking one nipple while thumbing the other, then switching. Gigi turned on her knees then and Danny felt her hot mouth around his cock.

"Oh fuck," he moaned. "Yes, baby."

It was Bree's turn to kiss him as he slid his hand in Gigi's hair and guided her mouth on his cock. He slid his other hand in Bree's hair and pulled as his tongue pushed in and out of her mouth.

Bree pulled back with a smile and kissed his chest all the way down. Both women were on their knees now, sucking and licking his cock.

"Fuck yes," he panted.

Bree took his balls in her mouth as Gigi deep-throated him.

"Fuck, stop, or I'm gonna come," he moaned.

They smiled at him as they kissed their way back up to his throat. Who to fuck first? Gigi was his choice. Those full, curvy hips were driving him wild.

"Come here, baby," he said. He lightly grabbed her and bent her over so he could slide in her. She leaned on the wall, holding on to one of the shelves.

"Yes, Danny, fuck me," she said.

He teased her with the tip as she moaned, then he thrust inside of her as she panted with pleasure.

"Holy shit, yes," she screamed. "Fuck me harder."

He pounded that beautiful pussy as he gripped her hips, sliding his hands up to her big full breasts and playing with her nipples. As he did, Bree grabbed his hair and pulled him into a deep kiss. He took one hand and slid it between Bree's legs, finger fucking her with quick, hard thrusts.

"Fuck, yes," she panted. She ran her hands up her chest to her perky breasts and squeezed her nipples. "Another finger, baby!"

He did as he was told and slid three fingers inside of her as he fucked Gigi deeply.

"Oh my God," Gigi moaned. "I'm gonna come."

"Come, baby," he ordered.

He pulled his fingers out of Bree and grabbed Gigi's hips, hard-fucking her like a man possessed.

"Like that baby?"

"Yes," she cried out. "Harder."

He slammed her even harder, his cock growing stiffer by the second as his balls slapped her clit and his cock drove deeper.

"You fucking like that?"

"God yes!" she panted. "I'm coming!"

"Come!"

"I'm coming!"

He fucked and fucked her until he felt her pussy tighten around his cock, squeezing it as she writhed, her come all over his cock.

"My turn," Bree ordered. She grabbed him and kissed him deeply as he gave one final thrust in Gigi, pulled out, then picked Bree up as she wrapped her legs around his waist. He opened the glass door and walked out to the bedroom. He dropped her on the bed and flipped her over.

"Yes, baby, yes!"

He spread her legs and positioned himself between them, slowly pushing the tip in and out until she was begging him to enter her.

"Fuck me!"

"Yes, baby," he said. He lifted her hips off the bed and drove his cock deep inside her.

"Yes!" she panted. "Harder."

He fucked her good and hard as he reached under her and grabbed her titties, stroking her nipples.

"Does that make you wanna come?"

"Yes!" She was writhing under him. "Fuck me!"

He kept one hand on her titty, rubbing her nipple, then slid the other one down to her pussy, rubbing her slick clit with a circular pressure as he pushed his cock deep inside her.

"Come, baby," he ordered.

"Yes, baby, yes!"

His orgasm gathered as he fucked her harder and harder.

"I'm coming!" she moaned.

"Come!"

He felt her pussy spasm around his thick, hard cock and he stayed right there, stroking her wetness until he was certain she was done, then he pulled out and jerked his cock until he came all over her back, spewing his hot, salty fluid over her butterfly tattoo.

"Fuck, that was good," he breathed. He reached for a tissue by the bed and cleaned off her back, then his hand, as Gigi walked out, a satisfied smile on her face.

"You're as good as Jenny said," Gigi murmured. She slid onto the bed and lay on her side as she smiled at him.

He laughed. "Well, thank you, I think."

Bree turned over and he helped her stand up.

"You deserve every accolade you get," she quipped. She kissed him on the cheek and laid down with Gigi on the bed.

He wasn't sure what to do so he smiled at both of them. Finally, Gigi tapped the bed.

"Come here, Danny," she said silkily. "We're not done with you yet."

He was living a porn movie right now and he wasn't sure what to think about that. But then again, women were more empowered these days to get the kind of sex they wanted when they wanted it. And that seemed to be the case here. He just didn't want to come off like an asshole.

"Can I buy you ladies dinner
first or—"

"Danny," Bree interrupted.
"Jenny already told us what a
gentleman you are. We get it."

"And we appreciate it," Gigi
said. She and Bree nodded at each
other then looked back to him.

"Yes, we do," Bree said.

"But this is just about the sex,"
Gigi said. "We're young. We're
having fun. Just—"

"Have some fun with us," Bree
interrupted. "And don't worry so
much about it. We're okay. We're
all okay and we're all adults here."

He glanced at them as they
smiled.

"But if you want, we can have a
conversation," Bree said.

"Can you just…" he hesitated.
"Can you tell me just a little about
yourselves?"

"I'm a nurse," Bree said. "And I
was in the same sorority as Jenny."

"Ditto that," said Gigi. "And I'm a dental hygienist. And you are?"

"I run a renovation business on the side with my buddies. Law clerk for a day job. Law school in two years."

"Oh, a future lawyer, no wonder you're so concerned," Bree said. She grinned. "You're a sweet guy."

"You really are," Gigi agreed. "Do you always follow the rules, Danny, the future lawyer?"

He smiled at her and shrugged. "I try to do what's right, yeah," he said. "But…it's nice to let go a little bit."

"Well, come here and let us help you relax," Bree said. She tapped the bed.

This time, he did as they said. Whatever this adventure was that Jenny had sent him on, he was up for it. He only had another two days for the renovation, and then he'd be gone. Until then, he was going to enjoy every second.

As he lay down between the beauties and felt their hands all over his body, he relaxed and sunk into a pleasure he'd never known before.

5

Pool Party

It was almost twilight as Danny finished up the renovation. He walked through the pool house and made sure every detail was perfect, every piece of tape removed and thrown away, every bit cleaned, every single thing in place. It looked beautiful.

He grinned. He wondered what Shannon would think when she got in the next morning and saw it. He hoped she liked it. Maybe he'd call her and find out if she did.

He walked out to the pool as nighttime started to close in. He turned on the gas torches and the gas firepit. The bright yellow flames against the darkening skies was beautiful. He flicked on the pool lights and admired the dark blue of the shimmering water. They were draining this pool in two days, so it was nice to see his finished work before they did.

"Looks great."

He smiled as he turned, knowing it was Jenny.

"Hey stranger," he said.

She laughed. "Sorry I had to bug out the other night. Work. They gave me a shot to be on-air. And that got me an audition an hour north of here. I'm leaving tonight."

"Ah," he said. He walked closer to her, a wide smile covering his face. "I think that's amazing, congratulations."

"Thanks," she said. She stepped closer to him until they were less than an inch apart. "I had a hell of a lot of fun with you."

He laughed. "Yeah, me too."

"I heard." She winked at him. A shimmer of heat passed between them.

"I know this was just for fun. And I'm good with that," he said. "But I'd still like to get your number if I could."

She grinned. "Yeah, that'd be okay."

She held out her hand. "Phone."

He unlocked his phone and gave it to her. Her blonde hair fell over her face as she entered her information. He reached over and swept it out of her face. She glanced up at him as she handed back his phone.

"You really are sweet, aren't you?" she asked.

He shrugged. "I don't know if sweet is the right word," he said. "But I was raised to respect women. And, at least for me, even if it's just a sexual relationship, a woman should still be treated well."

"I appreciate that, Danny," she said. "Feel free to text me anytime, okay?"

"I will," he said. She closed the distance between them and stood on her tiptoes as she gave him a sweet kiss.

"I have to go," she said quietly.

"Okay," he replied. She turned and walked away, then stopped and glanced back at him.

"By the way," she said. "I've set up a little surprise for you tonight. They should be here in a few minutes."

"Wait, what?" he asked. He looked around as she grinned. "They?"

"Danny, loosen up and have some fun," she said. She winked at him. "And don't forget about me, okay?"

"Oh, I promise you, I won't," he said. He grinned as she turned and walked away. "Good luck!"

She threw up a hand as she
walked through the pool house,
through the parking lot, and got in
her yellow bug. She started it up
and drive off as he gave one final
wave.

He glanced down at his phone
and laughed. She'd entered her
name as Jenny-fucking-Jones.

"Nice," he quipped.

"Are you Danny?"

He turned around to find three
beautiful women standing there in
varying degrees of nakedness. One
was brunette in a yellow bikini, one
was blonde in black bikini bottoms
and no top, and the third was
another blonde wearing nothing at
all.

"I'm definitely Danny," he said.
"And who are you?"

"Friends of Jenny," the brunette
said. "I'm Kayla. Former volleyball
player. This is Brynn and Bobbi.
Former cheerleaders."

The blondes grinned at him.

He just smiled because he didn't know what else to do. Jenny had gifted him a real live porn fantasy to try and loosen him up. It was working.

"Jenny said we should help you christen the pool now that you're all done," Brynn said. She smiled, then pulled off her black bikini bottoms and threw them aside.

"Yeah, she said you're a sweet guy who deserves a little fun," Bobbi agreed.

"And we'd love to help you out," Kayla cooed. She walked up to him and slowly removed her bikini, then took his hand and slid it between her legs. "And we don't need all that talkie-talkie."

He slid his fingers inside her wet slit and massaged her clit with his thumb.

"Yes," she moaned. He dipped his head down and pulled her

nipple into his mouth as he squeezed it with his free hand. "Fuck, mmm."

As he pleasured her sweet wetness, he felt four hands all over his body. Slowly, but surely, Brynn and Bobbi slid his clothes off him as he pleasured Kayla. When he was finally naked, Kayla took his hand and led him to the shallow end of the pool. All four of them slowly walked down the steps into the water. They had him sit on the second step.

"Come here," he ordered Kayla. She tasted delicious and he wasn't done with her. She stood in front of him, and he dove into her pussy, spreading her slit with his tongue and tasting her wetness. "Fuck you taste amazing."

He moaned as he felt Brynn and Bobbi take his cock in their hands and mouths. He reached one hand down and grabbed Brynn's hair, guiding her as she sucked his cock in her beautiful mouth.

"Fuck, yes," he murmured as he slurped Kayla's beautiful juice and swirled her clit in his mouth.

"Danny, yes," she panted. She grabbed his hair and swayed her hips in time with his tongue. He couldn't drink her down fast enough.

"Mmm, baby," he moaned.

"My turn," Brynn said as she stood next to Kayla.

"Yes," he whispered. He let go of Kayla and pulled Brynn next to him as he dipped his tongue between her legs. She was saltier and wetter and he lapped her up as Kayla and Bobbi worked his cock.

"I'm gonna fuck you," Kayla said.

"Yes, baby," he said as he looked right her while he slid his fingers deep inside Brynn.

"Oh God yes," Brynn said as he finger fucked her.

"Ride my cock," he ordered.

"Yes, baby," Kayla purred. She straddled him as he licked Brynn's sweet slit.

Kayla was gorgeous and her pussy was perfectly groomed. She grabbed his cock and massaged it, then used the tip to play with her entrance.

"Mmmm, fuck me," he said urgently. He needed his cock deep inside Kayla. She finally slid down his shaft as they both moaned with pleasure. "God yes, Kayla, fuck me."

She expertly rode his cock, driving her pussy against him, her wetness all over his cock and balls. Bobbi came up to him on the other side and he switched from Brynn to Bobbi.

Bobbi had the most exquisite breasts he'd ever seen. Perfect, full, with gorgeous pink nipples. He reached over and sucked her titties with wild abandon as Kayla banged her body against his. He thrust his fingers deep inside Brynn and fucked her slick opening quick, then slow.

All three women were moaning with pleasure as the chlorinated water sloshed all around them.

He dipped his mouth from Bobbi's perfect breasts to her sweet-smelling mound and dove in, opening her folds with his tongue and tasting her. She was sweet with an almond taste, and he couldn't stop coating his tongue with her sexy wetness. He swallowed it as she writhed with pleasure, grabbing his hair and riding her pussy on his mouth.

"Oh God," Kayla panted as she squeezed his cock and rode him. "I'm gonna come."

"Come," he ordered, pausing from Bobbi's pussy to spur her on. "Come all over my cock."

"I'm coming on your cock!"

"Yes, baby!" he panted. He could feel Kayla's pulsing orgasm as her wetness coated every inch of his stiff member.

"Fuck yes," she said with pleasure as she slowed her hips. When she'd taken everything she wanted she slid off his cock. He turned then to Bobbi. He wanted to fuck her deep and hard. He stood and backed her up to the edge, turned her around and bent her over the edge of the pool. He stood on the second and third steps, lifted her hips, and drove his cock deep inside her.

"Fuck me!" she yelled. He thrust hard and fast inside her amazing wetness, sliding his hands down her hips to her breasts and squeezing her nipples as she panted with pleasure. "I love your cock."

"You like that big cock in you baby?"

"Yes, baby, yes, fuck me!"

He gripped her titties and slammed that beautiful pussy as his balls banged against her clit. It was no surprise to him when she came quick and hard. He could feel how powerful her orgasm was as it gripped his cock in waves. He was close now, too.

He slowly pulled out as Bobbi turned and smiled at him in total relaxation and pleasure. Kayla joined her and they played with each other's titties and pussies as he turned to Brynn.

"Fuck me," she said.

He picked her up and she wrapped her legs around his hips.

"I'm on the pill," she said. "So you can come all you want in me."

"Fuck yes," he moaned.

He carried her out of the pool
and to one of the long lawn chairs.
He laid her down and she spread
her legs wide for him. He pulled
back to look at her.

"Fuck you're gorgeous, Brynn,"
he said.

"You know my name," she
whispered.

"Of course I do," he said.

"Fuck me," she ordered.

"Not yet," he teased. He dipped
his head and ate her salty pussy
with delight. She tasted
extraordinary. He pulled back and
waited until he caught her eye, then
he lightly slapped her pussy. Just
enough pressure to make her clit
tingle.

"Oh fuck," she gasped. "Do it
again."

He slapped her pussy again and
she gasped with pleasure.

"Fuck yes," she panted. He slapped her ass then, with a solid whack.

"Oh God, yes," she moaned. "Slap my ass, baby."

He slapped it again and as soon as he did, he spread her legs and drove his thick cock deep inside her.

"Yes!" she screamed. "Fuck me!"

He grabbed her legs and pounded her with everything he had. "Like that baby?"

"Yes, fuck, harder!"

He lifted her hips, changing the angle, and forcing his cock even deeper, a move that had her G-spot humming as he relentlessly thrust in and out of her.

"I'm gonna come," she moaned.

"I'm coming with you," he yelled.

He felt her pussy squeeze around his cock and he wanted to come inside of her. Coming inside of a woman was a fucking amazing feeling. But he'd always reserved it for someone he loved.

He quickly pulled out and jerked his cock until he came all over her stomach.

"Fuck," he said. His release was powerful and thick, covering most of her abdomen.

He laughed a little as he looked at her. "You're amazing."

"Thanks," she said. She smiled.

"Let me help you," he said. He stood and found a towel at the little amenities station, brought it back, and cleaned her up. When he was done, he helped her stand as Kayla and Brynn stepped out of the pool.

"Should we take this back to Jenny's?" Kayla asked.

He glanced at the three women. They were beautiful. And most men would think he was out of his mind for what he was about to say, but it had to be said.

"I don't think tonight, ladies," he said. "You're all amazing and this was…incredible. But I better say goodnight."

"Too bad," Brynn said. She shrugged as she walked away and gathered her things, followed by Bobbi. Kayla stayed back.

"You really are something," she said. "Jenny was right."

She smiled at him and he couldn't help but step to her and caress her arms, then give her a light kiss on the cheek.

"Thank you for such an amazing night," he said.

"No, thank you," she cooed. She gave him a wink and walked away. She quickly turned back and smiled. "I hope you got Jenny's number."

He grinned. "I did."

She gave him a knowing smile
and grabbed her things as the three
girls walked through the pool
house, out into the parking lot, and
into Jenny's condo.

He picked up all his clothes and
got dressed, then walked around
and shut everything off. Before he
shut off the final light, he looked
around at the work he'd done. It
really was good work.

He grinned, shut off the light,
and headed home.

6

Business or Pleasure?

Danny looked at his buddies and knew they were shocked into silence. Everything he'd done was something *they* would have done, not him. It was going to take them a minute.

It was Wolfe who spoke first.

"Dude," he said. "Fuck."

"I mean, I don't even know how to respond," Ben said.

"Me, either," Jack said. He shook his head and sat back. "I'm speechless."

They all just stared.

"Someday fucking say something," Danny said.

"The work was good. I saw the photos—"

"Not about that, Jack," Danny interrupted.

"Okay, look," Wolfe said. He sat up and leaned on his knees. "This is so unlike you. Are you okay?"

Wolfe would be the one to ask that question. They'd been friends for more than two decades; Wolfe knew him better than anyone.

"I just," Danny paused. "I'm always the good guy, you know? I just wanted to be—"

"Bad?" Ben asked. "Very, very bad?"

They all laughed as Ben made a sexy face. Danny picked up a football and tossed it at him. "Shut up, asshole."

Wolfe leaned back with a laugh. "Look man, you've always lived like a forty-year-old man. Even when we were ten," he said. They all laughed. "I'm glad to see you acted your age for once. And that you just enjoyed the sex for the sex, and you lived a little. Loosened up a bit.”

Danny nodded. “It felt good. To not have a plan. To just get in there and enjoy it. Plus, my God they were hot.”

“Holy shit, I need to meet Mads,” Ben said.

“I’ll take the blonde B’s,” Jack said. They all looked him questioningly. “Bobbi and Brynn, baby.”

They all laughed. Wolfe eyed him for a second.

“But you did get Jenny’s number, right?” Wolfe asked.

Danny nodded.

“So, not all just fun and games, then.”

Danny gave Wolfe a knowing smile. Yeah, his best friend could see through his tiny white lie. It had all been fun, and it was casual, but it had all started and ended with Jenny. He had taken care with her, because he hoped that maybe, someday, he might see her again.

"So, should we talk about our next project then?" Ben asked.

"That's mine," Jack said. "A log cabin. I'm already working on ordering the materials. A simple kitchen and living room update. Starts in two months, just after Thanksgiving. About a week to finish."

"Business or pleasure?" Wolfe asked. He raised his eyebrows.

Jack laughed. "Business. It was a man who hired me. Family cabin. He does have a daughter, though."

"He better hide her," Danny quipped.

They all laughed as they talked about their next projects and how they were already ten percent toward their financial goals—and loving every minute of it.

<u>**More to Come!**</u>

Danny's sexy story isn't over!
Keep reading the *Men Who
Renovate Erotic Series* to see what
happens to him, Jenny, and his sexy
friends! Wanna learn more about
the other men—Wolfe, Jack, and
Ben? Keep reading the *Men Who
Renovate Erotic Series* as they
build their business, enjoy sex, and
talk about it all!

Scan me

www.ingramcontent.com/pod-product-compliance
Lightning Source LLC
Chambersburg PA
CBHW031549310726
48971CB00008B/2682